Mélange

*Eclectic Renderings
of an
Enigmatic Consciousness*

Craig Mahler

Acknowledgments

I invite my readers to follow with me on the many journeys within my mind. You may see yourself or someone you know within the words. A few of the stories are true; others could be, while even others are ramblings conceived by my over-active imagination.

I would like to take just a minute to thank those who, without their gentle nudging, this book would never have been produced. There are nine in particular I need to acknowledge, my brothers and sisters. That's right, I'm one of ten, so you can just imagine what's rolling around inside my head. Without them, I would be an only child. (Or should I say, a lonely child). Either way, their antics are forever stuck inside my head just inching to come out.

My mother, what can I say other than, you are a saint for surviving as long as you did. She is and will always be loved. My lovely daughter and new found son are keeping things interesting for me right now. I do love them so.

Then there are my dearest friends, (Vincent, Susan, Jeff and Sue) without them you would probably be reading someone else's work.

Finally, there's the love of my life, Brenda. We met at our Thirty year high-school reunion, and I do mean met. Even though we spent three years roaming the same halls, we never once came across each other. We are making up for lost time. She has inspired me to pick up the pen again. Okay, I don't want to date myself, it's a keyboard. Anyway, she is why this eclectic collection of poems and stories are in your hands right now. And I want to thank you, for your support.

CONTENTS

Losing Faith	pg. 01	Shanty Town	pg. 37
Old Friends	pg. 05	A Picture's worth…	pg. 38
A Crystal Lighthouse	pg. 06	Tranquility on the Pontchartrain	pg. 41
A Mother's Poem	pg. 07	Repentance	pg. 42
The Adventure of Our Lives	pg. 08	Writer's Block	pg. 43
The Existence of Angels	pg. 11	All Tripped Out	pg. 44
Images of You	pg. 12	Deserted Fragments	pg. 47
Images of You in White	pg. 13	Mistletoe	pg. 48
Broken Toyz	pg. 14	A Wondering Eye	pg. 49
The Snow Bird	pg. 18	Tattered Edges	pg. 50
The Mourning Path	pg. 19	Sometimes	pg. 53
The Reality of Acceptance	pg. 20	Manchac Cypress	pg. 54
A Mardi Gras Tale	pg. 21	Nocturnal de Vieux Carre'	pg. 55
A Single Heart	pg. 24	My Trip to the Zoo	pg. 56
No Reservations	pg. 25	The Warrington Warehouse	pg. 58
Nature's Quilt	pg. 26	The Path	pg. 59
Bored Stiff / Board Stiff	pg. 27	One Final Tap for a Shining Star	pg. 60
Lingering Thoughts of You	pg. 35	Longing	pg. 80
A Father's Regret	pg. 36	Reunion of Strangers Love in Waiting	pg. 81
		Paradise	pg. 82

Copyright © 2013, 2018, 2024 by Craig Mahler

Cover art by Courtney Mahler

Poem Photos by Select Photographers from Free Use Photo Sites

All rights reserved. This book, or parts thereof, may not
be reproduced in any form without permission.

Library of Congress Cataloging-in-Publication Data

Mahler, Craig

Mélange – Eclectic Renderings of an Enigmatic Consciousness
by Craig Mahler

Printed in the United States of America

"I am sitting in the shadow of a Cross, tears laying tracks down my face as I witness this ceremony unfolding before me. Faith, our precious little angel, sleeps within God's embrace. Her mother gently brushes the hair from her brow as a spectrum of light beams through stained glass, caressing her face…

…a man of the cloth forms the sign of the Cross upon her forehead, anointing her with the Holy Spirit, asking God's forgiveness for her sins. Any sins put upon this Earth are not of her accord, for she is pure of heart."

This is not a foreshadowing of things to come, but a remembrance of the past. This is a story of a loss no one should ever have to endure, and it's one that must be told.

Losing Faith

I was a reporter for a small newspaper in the Deep South during the late Seventies. My editor wanted a different spin on how the youth of that time handled peer pressure, and how that related to their belief in God. I was surprised when I was given the assignment to cover a youth retreat, because I never was a huge believer in an all-knowing supreme being. How was I to know just how much this assignment would change my life? I was anticipating a group of bible pushing holy rollers, you know, a weekend of force-fed religion. But this was different. It was more about right and wrong and the consequences of one's actions. There were the occasional references to God, but most of all, these young teens learned about common sense.

The one good thing about that retreat was that I met my future wife, Karen. She was one of the counselors, and I knew instantly I wanted to spend my life with her. After a couple of months together, we decided to marry. I agreed to a big church wedding, only because I knew how important it was to her.

Over the years, we started to face the fact that having kids just wasn't meant to be. I had suggested fertility procedures to Karen, but she said if God wanted us to have children, it would happen. So we continued to live our lives together, alone. Then, soon after her fortieth birthday, Karen came home overwhelmed with joy. She was pregnant. I too was elated, but concerned about her having a child at her age. But everything turned out all right. Nine months later, we were blessed with a beautiful little girl. We named her Faith, because of my wife's undying belief.

Life was so wonderful sharing it with a young child. I even started going to church with my family. That led to me attending Sunday school classes, so that Faith and I could be baptized together. The wonder of a child softens your heart. It changes your priorities, and the way you look at life.

Birthdays flew by and soon Preschool was upon us. For the first time in her young life, Faith would have someone other than Karen or me to watch over her. As she walked down the hallway leading to her classroom, I could see the fear of the unknown in her big blue eyes. But Faith loved her new environment. All she could talk about were all the great new friends she had made in her school. That's why we were so surprised, after only a few months, we were called in for a conference with her teacher.

Faith had stopped playing with the other kids. She had crawled into a shell and seemed to be tired all of the time. Karen thought it might be the flu, and set up an appointment with the doctor. Test after test came back negative, yet Faith continued to get worse. Then the day came when we got the news no parent ever wants to hear; Faith had cancer. All I could do was pray for my little girl. Yes me, praying. My wife was furious. How could this be? How could a loving God do this to someone so young, so innocent? How ironic, the one person who taught me about God, now wouldn't allow his name to be mentioned in our house.

Karen had completely changed from that moment on. She even wanted to remove the Cross from over Faith's bed, but I insisted that it stay. I knew God would take care of our little angel.

Faith went through all the different medications and treatments. Some seemed to make Faith feel better, while others just made things worse. Karen and I even shaved our heads when Faith started to lose her hair, just so she wouldn't feel so different.

One of the best days of our lives was when we learned Faith was in remission. She progressively improved, and within six months, she was cancer free. And as Faith improved, so did Karen. We once again started attending church as a family. Karen was even happy to learn that she was pregnant once more. And now, with Faith fully recovered, and the new baby on the way, our home was a happy one once again. All seemed right in our world, until Faith started to get sick again. Within months, Faith was gone. The strain was too much for Karen to bear. At Faith's funeral, Karen went into premature labor, and was rushed to the hospital. I was torn between the burial of one child and the birth of another. I had to stay and see my little angel laid to rest.

By the time I finally made it to the hospital, Grace had been born. Within an hour's time, I had buried a daughter and had become a father once again. But the emotion of grief for Faith and the overwhelming joy for Grace couldn't prepare me for the shock I would soon have to face. There were complications during delivery. Karen had passed away. If not for the precious little being I held in my arms, I would have given up.

This is not the end of my story, but the beginning of a new life, one with Faith. You see my daughter Grace is all grown up and she has been blessed with a daughter of her own, which she named Faith, in honor of her sister's memory.

I am sitting in the shadow of a Cross, tears laying tracks down my face as I witness this ceremony unfolding before me. Faith, our precious little angel, sleeps within God's embrace. Her mother gently brushes the hair from her brow as a spectrum of light beams through stained glass, caressing her face. She releases the softest of cries as a man of the cloth forms the sign of the Cross upon her forehead, anointing her with the blessings of the Holy Spirit, asking God's forgiveness for her sins. Any sins put upon this Earth are not of her accord, for she is pure of heart.

I know in my heart that my wife, Karen and my daughter, Faith, are smiling down upon us as we celebrate this sacrament of life, this Baptism of faith.

Faith is never lost, it surrounds you, it fills you and it remains forever within your soul, embrace it!

Old Friends

As the mirror reveals each new line
and every gray the years bring on,
I remember the promises.
We said our farewells,
with every intention of keeping in touch.
But the calls, like the distance between us,
grew further apart.
As we drifted into our new lives,
I could never fill the void
of those I had left behind.
As I now near the twilight of my
existence I desperately attempt
to recapture memories lost.
But just like my youth, these too seem to fade.
I yearn to revisit those times once more,
for a gathering of those who have passed,
to be once again, with Old Friends.

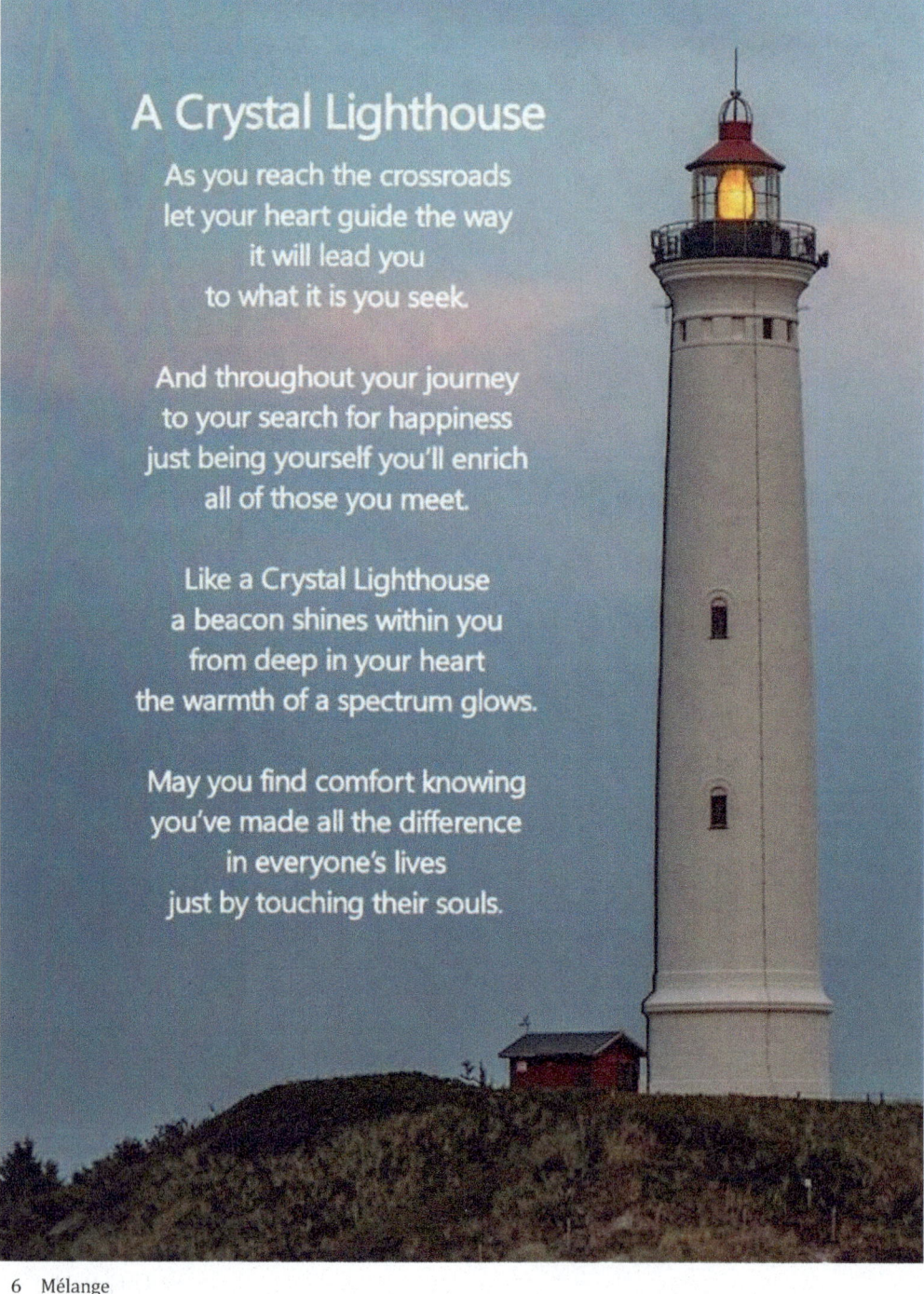

A Crystal Lighthouse

As you reach the crossroads
let your heart guide the way
it will lead you
to what it is you seek.

And throughout your journey
to your search for happiness
just being yourself you'll enrich
all of those you meet.

Like a Crystal Lighthouse
a beacon shines within you
from deep in your heart
the warmth of a spectrum glows.

May you find comfort knowing
you've made all the difference
in everyone's lives
just by touching their souls.

A Mother's Poem

You amaze me with your
ability to molds one's life
and nurture it through
its formative existence

You overwhelm me with your
unselfish generosity
and enormous influence
of strength you instill

You inspire me with your
Undying faith in God
That has created such
A tender loving being

I thank him every day for
the precious wonder of you

The Adventure of Our Lives

We always traveled together, it was safer that way. You never knew what was next, but you instinctively knew it was going to excite you. That was the whole idea of taking this wild ride. My fellow travelers and I had attempted this trip once before, but it turned out disastrous. One of us had gotten separated from the rest and was taken away by a giant rodent. You may think I'm crazy or that I had hallucinated the whole thing, but I swear it happened. I must confess, we were all out in the blistering sun for a long time, but that had nothing to do with what I saw.

This trip started off just like the last. The six of us were floating down a winding murky river in old hollowed-out tree trunks. We were being followed by tiny ripples on the water's surface. It served warning that a crocodile was in waiting. His eyes were glazed over, staring intensely toward his next meal. He was patiently waiting for someone to mistakenly allow their hand to slip over the edge. This was just the beginning of a long journey in our quest for adventure.

For the last couple of minutes we could hear the ever-increasing rhythmic beatings coming from just around the next bend. This could only mean trouble. We tried to slow our makeshift canoes, but the current had taken over. The thunderous beating continued to vibrate within our skulls. As we rounded the bend, there was nothing. No one was there. There were only footprints in the sand. Then, the drums stopped. From beyond the brush, a hail of tiny darts zipped over our heads. We huddled down for cover until we had floated past the turn. None of us had gotten hit, but we were all shook up pretty bad.

Leaving our canoes behind, we traveled by foot toward our next destination. The next leg of our journey was to scale the big white mountain. But it was a long walk away. And the sun was already beating us down. There were going to be many distractions ahead that would keep us from our goal to find the illusive mammoth creature. And we didn't want the same thing to happen to us that happened on the last trip, so we took a well-deserved break.

We would come across small villages of strange people, with Bazaars and marketplaces where you could trade for treasures from foreign lands. There was also an old mine where we encountered an elderly prospector. He swore that you could still pick up gold right off the ground. He led us through the mine in an old dilapidated cart. Its wheels would barely stay on the tracks as we descended deep into the darkness. As the cart moved faster, we all grabbed for the break handle, but it wasn't there, neither was the prospector. He must have fallen out on the last turn. We were left to ourselves in total darkness. That's when a beam of light appeared, and it was leading us closer to the end of our lives. Just when we all had started to pray for forgiveness, the cart abruptly stopped. A wooden door bursts open to reveal that we were once again spared a cruel and horrible death.

It was getting late in the day, and we still weren't any closer to our quest. We had been told by the villagers that the creature could be found on the other side of the great White Mountain. There was still the long hard trek to its summit ahead of us. Hours later, we had succeeded in our task of ascending the winding trails to its crest. The trip down from the peak was worth the whole journey up. As we reached the bottom of the mountain, we all embraced each other at the realization that our adventure was almost at its end. So we thought.

Someone had spotted the massive rodent heading toward a nearby hamlet. We cautiously stalked our prey. Just when we were about to pounce, someone grabbed our arms. In disbelief, the whole bunch of us were taken from the area. We were led off, through one of the villages, toward the gate that surrounded it. As we passed under the immense opening, there was a loud voice radiating throughout our heads, "Can you kids try not to get lost the next time we come to Disney World?"

The Existence of Angels

They're in the compassion you feel
in the way that you live
the glow of your being
comfort you give

They're in the softness of a touch
in the twinkle of an eye
the warmth of a smile
release of a sigh

They're in the tears of one's sorrow
in the length of a prayer
the reassurance of Faith
love that we share

They're in the depths of your soul
In the kindness you do
the heart of an Angel
exist within you

Image of You

From the moment of you birth as you opened your eyes
to the sound of your cry as you started to talk.
From the curve of your mouth as you created a smile
to the strength of your will as you struggled to walk.
From the volume of your voice as you screamed out a cheer
to the wave of your arms as you learned how to swim.
From the applause for your performance as you starred in a play
to the grace of your form as you flew through the gym.
From the gentle tiny infant who's life just began
to the tender young woman who's learning to live.
From the images of you embedded deep in my heart
To the promise I make of all the love I can give.

Images of You
In White

I see God's greatest miracle
wrapped in white linen,
the stretch of your body
as you took your first breath.
A tender young infant
held ever so gently,
the reassurance of others,
your sins put at rest.
The color of purity
amongst a sea of children,
your tiny voice abounds,
as it stands out alone.
You graciously accepting
the body of Christ,
the bread of life,
into your own.
One image of you
is still but a dream,
you walk down the isle
to start a new life.
A veil of fine lace,
the color of snow,
in front of our lord,
you become a new wife.
These images of you fill my heart,
Like the commitment
you've made to God's only Son.
I wish you happiness forever,
for your journey through life
has just begun.

Broken Toyz

It was late afternoon on a warm June day in a small rural community just outside of New Orleans. Miss Posey, a middle-aged woman, dressed in her Sunday best, casually travels down the winding river road that would bring her to the home she must visit today. She turns unto an oak lined drive, just along the grounds of the local cemetery. Once at the home, she slowly ascends the steps, hesitating briefly, as she is startled by a sudden flash of light. It is only then that she noticed a man sitting next to the railing of the front porch. She didn't recognize him, even though she knows him well, as do the rest of the people in this small town. Everyone here is aware of the pain associated with this man. She rushes into the home and peers through the shears covering the oval glass of the front door.

The man had just lit a cigarette and was reaching for his lighter that had just slipped from his hand. He seemed too preoccupied to even acknowledge anyone else was there. His eyes were transfixed on the porch of a modest country home across the way. There was a young boy, who appeared to be about twelve or so, building what seemed to be a fortress with assorted letter blocks. It looked as if he was trying to reenact a battle with an eclectic array of toy soldiers.

As the boy played, his father returned from work and headed directly into their home, completely oblivious to his son's presence, even though the boy had told him hello. Moments later, the boy hears his father's voice radiating through the house, the volume ever increasing as he returns to the porch. A long shadow falls over the boy's fortress as his father crosses behind him. Only then does his father notice his son sitting there. His dad just couldn't understand why his son wasn't playing ball like the other kids his age. No, Matthew was playing with an old tin soldier and a bunch of toy blocks.

Matthew hears his mother announcing that dinner was ready. And as his dad heads into the house, Matthew is told to pick up and come inside to eat. The boy meticulously returns each block and soldier to its pre-designated location in an old shoe box. The boy's favorite was a small tin soldier he had received from his late grandfather. He was just about to place the soldier on top when he hears his father's scream, "I told you to come inside and eat!" At that same instant, Matthew's toys are flung across the porch by a swift kick of his father's foot, shattering them against the front of the house.

Matthew frantically searches the fragments for the Napoleonic man he cherishes so much. You see, it reminds him of everything good in life. It reminds him of the only man who showed him any sought of love, his grandfather. He discovers the soldier, bent in two, lying next to a potted plant. And as he caresses it, like one would a wounded bird, he hears the encouraging sound of his mother's voice telling him it will be okay.

The man on the steps is mesmerized by the scene he has just witnessed. He gets up and lights another cigarette as he prepares to take a walk down the path to the river road. As he returns, he passes Matthew and Courtney, the boy's friend, on their way to the local fair. A few hours later, the man sees the young couple returning, hand in hand. Matthew seems to be nervous. Maybe it's because he is anticipating what would soon be his first kiss. Even though it's just on the cheek, it's just what the boy needed to help him forget his troubles at home.

The man notices, through the window, Matthew's father lying on the couch. And even though he's obviously out to the world, Matthew's dad manages to balance a half empty beer bottle between his outstretched fingers and the floor. The television seems to be pulsating as its glow is projected across the living room wall. The man sees a shadow crossing the room towards the television. It's Matthew, and as he reaches to turn it off, a shower of sparkles strays past his eyes. Matthew looks down and sees broken glass on the floor and instinctively reaches for the pain coming from the back of his head, and as his father stumbles out of the room, Mathew's mother hurries to the boy's assistance.

Matthew's mother has had enough. She starts to pack the car, in hopes of taking Matthew away from this abusive man. She tells Matthew to go to the car and wait, but Matthew heads to his room. There was something he just couldn't leave behind. He just couldn't relinquish it, not while there was still the pain of his father's so called love. This was the only thing that gave him the strength to handle all the abuse. While standing next to his night stand, Matthew hears the horrific sound of his mother's scream. He rushes to the kitchen and sees his mother slumped over the sink with a rag pressed to her eye, his father standing over her.

Matthew knew this could go on no longer. He pushes his father back and to the floor. His dad staggers to his feet and slaps the boy with the back of his hand, expecting Matthew to back down. But Matthew pushes his father again. This time his dad punches Matthew across the face, spinning him around and through the jalousie glass door behind him. Matthew lays lifeless amongst a bed of shattered glass, his mother desperately attempting to revive him.

The whine of an approaching siren rivets the man sitting on the steps across the street. He is left emotionally exhausted by the realization of what he has just encountered. The man unconsciously heads up the steps leading to the home where he had been sitting all this time. As the door opens, he is greeted by Miss Posey. She gently hugs him, as if to comfort him somehow. After their embrace, she heads down the hallway, her eyes never straying from the room at its end. The man follows, and as he enters the room, he notices her standing beside a casket.

At its edge sits a freshly inscribed plaque with the words, *"We must forgive to mend the broken."* He gazes down at the fragile being lying before him and thinks how ironic those words truly are. He places his hand in the casket, then turns to leave, pausing momentarily in the foyer to sign the Guest Registry.

Miss Posey kneels to pay her respects and is shocked to find, just inside the casket, a tiny tin soldier. She rushes down the hall to the Registry in a desperate attempt to find the identity of this troubled man. There, in total disbelief, Miss Courtney Posey finds but one word, **"Matthew."**

The Snow Bird

Within the dense pale forest,
with its branches straining
from a blanket of virgin white snow,
a tree stands precariously alone.
Within this harsh dead of winter
comes the deafening cry of new life,
as a tiny young bird
beckons for the sounds of its own.

It is but an ivory shadow
amongst the pearl covering,
wallowing against the winter winds,
balancing ever so gently upon its perch.
May this semblance of God's tiniest creature,
with its undying will to endure,
help find deep within you
the strength for which we all search.

The Mourning Path
St. Louis Cemetery #2

A tattered Calico traverses the crumbling corridor
dissecting a row of dilapidated sacred structures,
each uniquely indistinguishable from the next.

The wind carries an eerie refrain
as it whistles through the splintered stones,
white-washed to harbor their degeneration.

There's a fragrant stench of wilted petals
lying dormant in stagnant waste;
This potpourri of nature's compost
resonates from the marred receptacles
lining this mourning path.

Picket shadows serve no comfort
from the unbearable fervor
as it bakes these palaces of the deceased.

Irreverent voyagers marvel at its spectacle,
congregating within the blighted vestibules,
ignoring the pleas of sacrilege,
all to capture images for their own posterity.

Exit this city of the dead,
allow the mourners their serenity due.
Bestow the departed their wanted peace
and leave them to their gentle rest.

The Reality of Acceptance

Acceptance is an affliction festering within the minds of the hordes,
within those who fail to accept their own imperfections.
I am far too familiar with the pains of ridicule
and my own unwarranted determination of acceptance
into a society that belittles those who are atypical.
I was once absorbed by my own persistence,
my own self-pity, my own ignorance.
We each possess our own abnormalities, some visually apparent,
others lay dormant within a conceited mind.
I am repulsed by those who, under scalpel,
alter their guise, merely to appease society.
In their distorted reality, acceptance is paramount.
I lament for those whose impairments
encumber a comparatively normal existence.
Normality is relative to one's own mind,
as is the sad reality of being accepted by others.

A Mardi Gras Tale

We could hardly believe it was just before dawn,
when Mom woke us up to have our costumes put on.
Dad packed up the Mercury and we headed uptown,
I was a cowboy and my brother a clown.
Two sisters wore pink tights, another wore black,
my face, stuck to the window as I sat in the back.
Dad whispered, "CALM DOWN," in a very loud tone,
as one sister screamed out to leave her alone.
After driving forever, we came to a stop,
"You can't go this way," we were told by a cop.
We couldn't cross St. Charles, is what we were told,
the parade was before us, with all its purple and gold.
This krewe was never on time, except on that day,
scattered rain was the forecast, so they got on their way.
We had missed the King's float, and to our surprise,
the largest crowd ever was in front of our eyes.
A wall of wood ladders stood where we should be,
we pushed ourselves forward, so that we could see.
We would end up behind this extremely huge man,
which really messed up our bead catching plan.

"It's the Budweiser Clydesdale's," I heard the man yell,
and then he would curse, "What the Hell is that smell?"
The horse did its business, which is stuck to my shoe,
what made matters worse; my brother had to go too.
"I have to go bad," is all he would say,
The nearest location was two blocks away.
I stood there forever, my brother in tow,
we had waited so long, he just couldn't go.
By the time we returned the parade had passed by,
my brother fell down and started to cry.
Mom fed us some lunch, and said, "In a while, the
truck floats would pass." and we started to smile.
There were beads in the trees and doubloons all around,
my brothers and sisters were all over the ground.
We stuffed all our bags; we could fill them no more,
time had flown by; it was a quarter-to-four.
Dad packed up the car and Mom counted our heads,
by the time we got home we were thrown in our beds.
I'll never understand how we did it back then,
Two weeks of parades with a family of ten.
The year's not important; it was a long time ago,
if you ask all my siblings if it happened just so,

You'll get ten different stories, all told their own way,
of what happened to them on that Mardi Gras Day.
The years have flown by and now that we've grown,
we come back every year with kids of our own.
Once, we changed our location and soon we would learn,
it was just not the same out on Vets and Severn.
We're back on St. Charles where this all began,
there are still all the ladders and that same giant man.
With all the madness around us, we lounge in our chairs,
our kids are in chaos, but who really cares?
A child has to go now, and it just might be mine,
so, you'll have to excuse me, I'll be standing in line.

A Single Heart

As sirens echo through the dim sterile halls
a man lies dormant, his life sustained by lines
nourishing him with tempering moments of existence.
With unwavering Faith he awaits the matching
that will replace his weakened heart,
for he has given his all for this single miracle.
Late into this troubled night, an awakening will occur
as a young girl is rushed from an adjoining passage.
Before the man is ushered toward his new beginning
he unselfishly offers that cherished organ
so that life can flourish within a little angel,
for her being would cease without his saving grace.
Now, each year of her new life, a candle is lit.
Her birthdays belong with this stranger,
for they are forever joined by a single heart.

No Reservations

A woman stands before me,
tears flowing from swollen sockets,
streaks shadowed by a thin veil.
A full congregation,
tissues in hand, for some will weep.
Their eyes transfixed forward,
I am the focus of their attention.
A pastor's offering,
beckoning a wanted response.
In this vast Cathedral
sighs echo.
What eerie silence within this moment
before the words, "I do."

Nature's Quilt

A congregation hovers effortlessly in chaotic unison,
then plummets within a cool graceful wisp.
Anticipation abounds, for soon upon this flowing ridge
there will be a gathering,
an assembly of the descending flock.
An infinite palette of rusted hues
shimmers through their transparent membranes,
each leaf uniquely indistinguishable.
They lie in a distinct disorder upon this panoramic canvas,
a precise indiscriminate pattern to its weave.
With one final brush of an Autumn's wind,
we are offered the warmth of Nature's quilt
and this serene vision of its journey into Fall.

Bored Stiff Board Stiff

CHAPTER ONE
Inheriting the Reigns

I"m sitting in the overly plush office of my recently departed father, surrounded by my so-called family. Directly across from us, in the huge leather chair my dad had occupied for the last thirty years, sits an extremely zealous estate shyster by the name of Hugo Stuffitt. We were all there for the reading of my father's will. That is, all but my oldest brother, Max Jr. He is currently residing up state, three years left on a ten to twelve. There was some kind of small problem, a small misunderstanding over some unpaid taxes. That's something I would rather not discuss at this particular time and place. There are more important matters at hand, namely which one of my siblings will take control of the family business. Personally, I"m betting on Joey, my youngest brother and my father's little pet.

Ever since Joey was old enough to wipe his own butt, dad would take him along and show him the ropes. By the time he had graduated high school, Joey was named Assistant to the Vice-president of Operations, who just so happened to be my older sister, Vera. She's a trip. Not only does she expect to get the head position, she's already decided to hire Oscar to take over her job when she moves up the ladder. Oscar is her half-witted, gold-digging, way too young for her boyfriend.

Let us not forget the brother to my right, Walter. Walter's the vulture of the family, living off anybody and everybody he can. He's someone who's never had a job and never wants one. As long as someone pays the way, he's just fine. He has actually lived with every one of us more times than I can count. And now that dad has passed away, Walter has taken over his home. He virtually lives in the hot-tub out back with one of his many girlfriends.

Then there's me. My name is Charlie. I too have had my share of problems. Twenty years ago I got into a huge argument with my dad over why I didn't want to work for him, and we probably hadn't said ten words to each other since. I wanted to make something of myself, on my own. And the fact that it took me years to achieve what I wanted didn't make things any better between us. But I know he worried about me. Before my mother passed away, she would tell me that my father would ask how I was doing. I guess we were both too stubborn to admit our feelings toward each other.

Anyway, we are all sitting here staring at Mr. Stuffitt as he opens his briefcase to reveal a single piece of paper. On it is my father's last wishes. The first to be mentioned was Walter, and the son-of-a-gun got the house, and nothing else. There were a few small stipulations he must follow. One was, he could never sell the house. Another was he had to get and keep a job to pay for the upkeep. If not, the house goes to Joey.

Joey gets twenty-five percent of dad's stocks and the title of Vice-President of Operations. That's right. He gets Vera's job, which meant only one thing, she got what she wanted. We all started to congratulate her when the lawyer intervened. There was one slight problem. Not only did she not get the job, she was demoted to sorting the mail. There was something dad knew about Vera, but didn't tell anyone else. The only things she did get were some of my mother's jewelry that dad had saved for her. Max Jr. got some shares that went directly to cover his past taxes, with interest.

    I got the rest, the cars, the beach house and the JOB. That's when all hell broke loose. I just sat back in disbelief as Vera went nuts. She was all over the lawyer, threatening to sue the estate. Joey, on the other hand, congratulated me and said he looked forward to working with me. That shocked me even more. Joey and I never got along. I really hadn't got along with any of my siblings. I couldn't understand why he wasn't mad. I guess he just accepted dad's wishes, yea right!

CHAPTER TWO
Taking the Reigns by the Balls: Literally

My troubles were just beginning. I soon found out what my dad knew about Vera. The company was in shambles. When my dad first got ill, Vera had over spent the company's budget by two-thirds. There was an inventory problem and everyone above the janitors was getting over paid. Within two months of taking over, I had tightened up the business to an acceptable level. The family still wasn't happy. They weren't going to see any dividends for a while. But the company was on line to make a profit by the end of the year.

My personal life was also turning around. I was once married to the Wicked Witch of Oz. She was and still is a blood-sucking demon out to get every penny I ever or will have for the rest of my life. As much as I hate that woman, she did give me a beautiful daughter before talking me into getting a vasectomy. That was the biggest mistake I've ever made, because, now I'm engaged to someone four years older than my eighteen year old daughter. And my fiancé wants to have kids, lots of kids. So now we've planned for me to have the even more painful procedure of a reversal. The things we do for love.

My fiancé suggested the overly expensive doctor, I. M. Studdley to do the operation. He decided that I should be put to sleep for the operation. I really didn't like that term, "put to sleep." That's when things started to get bad. Yeah, it gets worse. I remember counting backwards until I got to the number ninety-two. After that, there was nothing. That was until I heard a familiar voice say, "How could this have happened?"

I was still in the hospital, days after the operation, laid out in a bed. I could feel what seemed like a huge mound around my private area rising up from under my covers. It must have looked like Mt. St. Helens before it erupted. I say must have, because I couldn't see a thing, I was in a coma. Let me tell you one thing right now, people in comas can hear you. Here I was ease-dropping on every word said in my room. That voice, the one that seemed so concerned about me, it was Vera. It was obvious she didn't think I could hear her. She couldn't wait for me to croak. She would visit every day just to see if I was getting any worse. She even had the nerve to tell her Guido boyfriend how she planned to take over after I'm gone.

My brother Joey wasn't any better. He was the one who said he looked forward to working with me. He was looking forward all right, for me to flat-line right out of his way to the top. Oscar's daughter, Samantha, even came by to see if she might profit from my demise. Walter, the vulture, was the only one not to visit me, but he did call. I overheard a nurse tell him I might not make it through the week. Walter was so concerned about me; he took the time to ask the nurse out on a date. What a bunch of ass-holes. I have never been a religious man, but I prayed to God to let me live long enough to take care of my loving family. And I do mean take care of.

Even my soon-to-be ex fiancé only came by twice. I say "ex," because I found out she was messing around with Dr. Studdley, the quack she suggested in the first place. Can you believe they had the gall to make out at the foot of my bed while I was trying to listen to the soaps?

Reckoning time was quickly approaching. After two weeks of this crap I opened my eyes, and the only one there was my daughter. Chloe had stayed by my side when no one else was around. She never could stand my family, so she would go down the hall until they all would leave. You really do find out who cares when things get rough.

CHAPTER THREE
When it Reigns, it pours

I couldn't wait to get back to the office. I wanted to see just how two-faced everyone would be. But first things first, I had to deal with my fiancé. She played the, I'm happy you're well routine, until I showed her a video of her and Dr. Stud-master doing the nasty in our bedroom. I guess she forgot about the camera she had put there for her kinky video fetish. And how it got aired on the internet is beyond me. It is a shame that Dr. Studdless lost his license. Maybe he can get a job in the porn industry. From what I saw, he might come up a little short. I didn't say that, did I?

Next was my sister, Vera. I decided, since she worked in the mail room, I would send myself a letter. Yes, I said myself. I knew Vera was reading all of my mail, so inside one of them I left this note:

"Dear former Vice-President and future
unemployed mail clerk,
YOU'RE FIRED!!!
Your loving brother, Charlie."

Joey was a little harder to get rid of. He was smarter than the rest, so I had to let him hang himself. The whole time I was in the hospital, Joey was concocting a way to take over my job. He tried to make it look like I was embezzling company funds. But he screwed up when he moved money around while I was in my coma. The company auditors had caught the problem and waited for my return before contacting the proper authorities. I guess he wasn't as smart as he thought. I am currently trying to arrange for Joey to be near Max Jr. Wouldn't that be nice?

Last but not least, what to do with Walter? I thought this over and over again, and I came to the conclusion, he didn't do a thing. He was just being Walter. So I gave him a job. He is the new Assistant, to the Assistant of the Vice-President of Operations, which just so happens to be my daughter, Chloe.

I received a letter from Joey today. Max Jr. introduced him to Bruno, that special kind of friend you don't want to have while showering in prison. I do hope they are getting along. They deserve each other, Max Jr. and Joey, not Bruno.

Well, that's my story. Oh, I almost forgot. If you're ever on What-d-hell-r-u-doing-here Road at three a.m. and you need gas, stop at the Suds-and-Go and say hi to their new assistant to the assistant night manager, Vera.

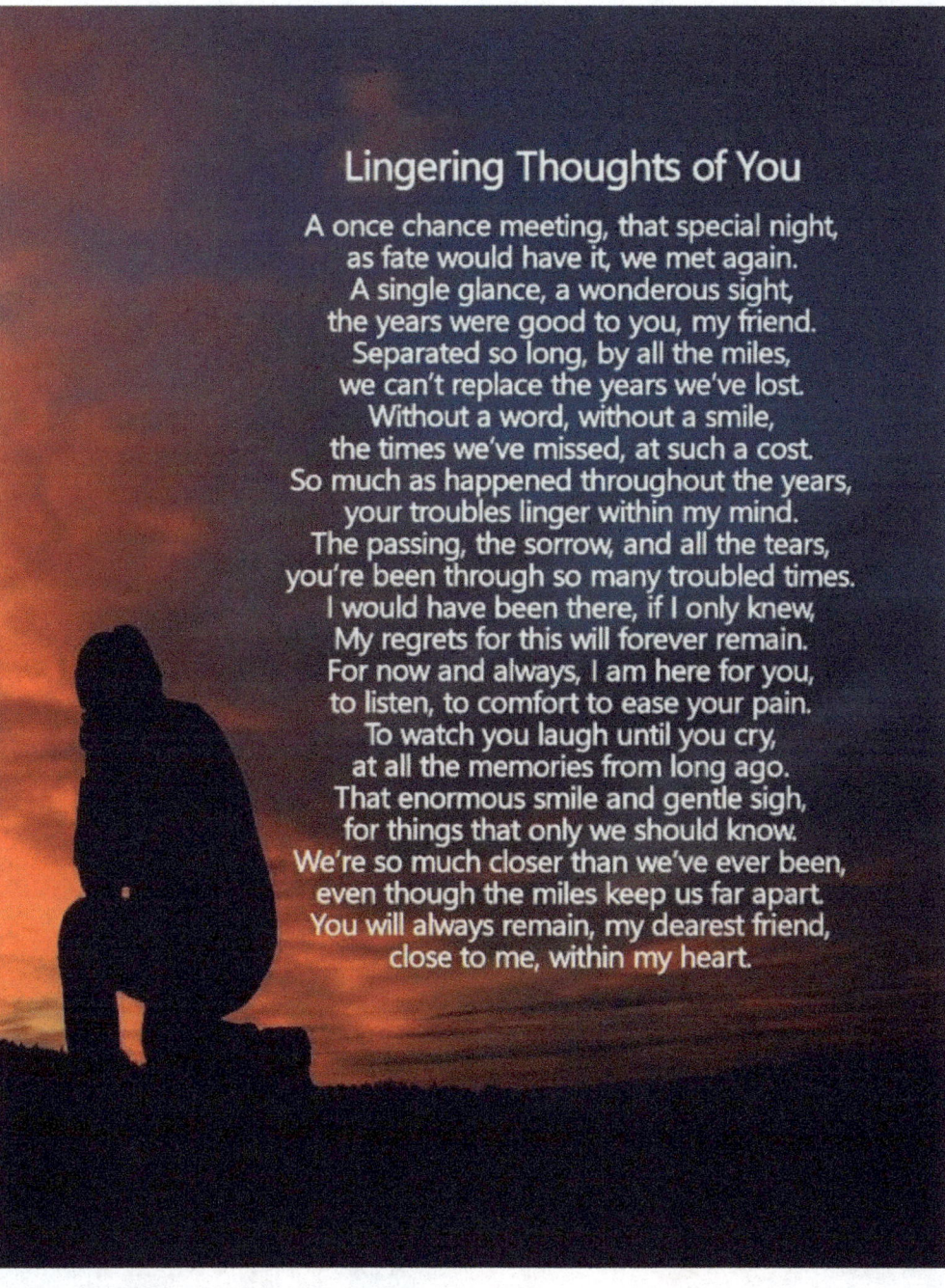

Lingering Thoughts of You

A once chance meeting, that special night,
as fate would have it, we met again.
A single glance, a wonderous sight,
the years were good to you, my friend.
Separated so long, by all the miles,
we can't replace the years we've lost.
Without a word, without a smile,
the times we've missed, at such a cost.
So much as happened throughout the years,
your troubles linger within my mind.
The passing, the sorrow, and all the tears,
you're been through so many troubled times.
I would have been there, if I only knew,
My regrets for this will forever remain.
For now and always, I am here for you,
to listen, to comfort to ease your pain.
To watch you laugh until you cry,
at all the memories from long ago.
That enormous smile and gentle sigh,
for things that only we should know.
We're so much closer than we've ever been,
even though the miles keep us far apart.
You will always remain, my dearest friend,
close to me, within my heart.

A Father's Regrets

I realized far too late the times lost,
those moments I couldn't spend with you.
I wasn't there to hold your hand,
those times when you needed me to.
The years have somehow passed us by,
our visits together grow further apart

I cherish each moment we share together,
but as you leave, it tears my heart.
You will always be my little Angel,
this image of you will never grow old.
You've grown into this precious woman,
the only one who fills my soul.
My love for you has never wavered,
it remains as strong as it's ever been.
I can only tell you, that I miss you
until the time we're together again.

Shanty Town

The dead of children's eyes burn through the soul,
their hunger tears the heart from its cavity.
Cheeks sunken as skin hangs from the bone,
their out-stretched arms crying for deliverance.
You would weep, if not for your crusted sockets,
for moisture is a cherished commodity.
From opulence and prosperity, we are left to scavenge
barren fields for spoiled fruit and wilted leaves.
These few morsels are to be our only subsistence.
This crash has laid waste to our destitution.
Each day emulates the last,
as do the cars rumbling along the rails
past this desolate hovel town.

A Picture's worth...

I'm sitting in coach on a long flight back to Chicago from New Orleans, desperately trying to come up with an excuse why I haven't completed my latest assignment. The man sitting next to me asked if the photo I was holding was that of my wife. I only wish. This woman was the reason I was going to be in so much trouble. I handed him the photo, and as we leaned back in our seats for the long journey home, I told this stranger my plight.

I'm a photojournalist and I was in town to cover the annual Jazz and Heritage Festival. I wasn't supposed to be there. The original photographer came up sick after just two days. My guess is he spent too much time sipping Hurricanes at Pat O'Brien's. Either way, I was on my way to New Orleans.

My flight there was on its final approach just before landing. In the distance I could see the Mississippi winding its way along the city's edge. The Big Easy wasn't as big as I had imagined. Sure, there were the tall buildings of downtown, but not as many as I'm used to seeing. Here it was, Monday afternoon, and I had missed the whole first weekend of the festival. Being who I was, I had received a whole bunch of free tickets and back stage passes to every local event for the next seven days. The only problem was; I don't do concerts. My normal assignment was covering Chicago area politicians. This was a whole different ball game. I knew nothing about the music scene. Monday night was spent reading about who the artists were, where and when they were playing and how I was going to get interviews with them. It was a nightmare. I didn't know what I was going to ask them, even if I got the chance.

Sleep was definitely out of the question. Bright and early Tuesday morning I headed to the free mini-festival going on along the Riverwalk. All of the artists were locals, but surprisingly, they were very good. I interviewed the ones I thought were interesting and took a few photos for the story. While I changed lenses to take some crowd reactions, I noticed this stunning creature standing just a few feet away. She was breathtaking. With her looks, there was no way she was there alone. After taking a few shots of the crowd, I slowly worked my lens toward this beauty. She started to laugh when she realized I was taking way too many photos of her. I eased the camera down from my face to apologize, but she was gone. I spent the rest of the day searching for her, but she was no where to be found.

The next couple of days I attended the nightly concerts and tried my best to interview the bands, but my mind was on that woman. Just when I was about to give up on finding her, she showed up in my lens again. This time it was at the Jazz Fest. I was up on the big stage taking crowd shots, when I spotted her. She was just a few feet away, so it seemed. She was actually so far into the crowd, without my zoom I would never have made out her face. As fast as I had found her, I had lost her again.

I was telling one of the other photographers about this woman, when he came up with an idea. He knew this guy, who knew this guy that could put her image up on the big screen in front of the stage. I just so happened to have her picture in my bag. Every couple of minutes her face showed up, thirty feet tall, for everyone to see. And at the bottom of it was written, "Come back stage!" I waited for what seemed like an eternity. But after three days of absolutely no sleep, I passed out. When I finally came to, I was in the first aid tent, with the picture of this woman lying on my chest. I sat up and there she was, standing at the edge of the cot. Her hands were on her hips, and she looked mad. She wanted to know what was going on. After explaining how much I went through just to meet her, she softened up. I must have impressed her. She said no one had ever done anything that crazy before. We finally introduced ourselves, and I asked her if she wanted to hang out back stage and meet some of the artist.

We ended up talking for hours, and after the festival shut down for the day, I invited her to accompany me to the next night time concert. She accepted and wrote her name and number on the back of the photo and told me to call her. We went on to spend the rest of the weekend together. By the time I was supposed to go back to Chicago, I had already decided that I wanted to spend the rest of my life with her. We had one last night together, falling asleep in each other's arms. When I opened my eyes from that peaceful sleep, her image was all I could see, all thirty feet of it. I was still at the Jazz Festival, in the first aid tent. I had hallucinated it all. She had never showed up. My chance for happiness had passed me by. All I had was this photo of her.

Just as I finished telling this stranger my story, I realized he had fallen asleep. When I took the photo from his hand I noticed something on its back. It was a name and number, and the words, "Call me!" She had showed up after all. Now I'm desperately trying to come up with an excuse why I'm taking a connecting flight back to New Orleans. Do you think my boss will understand? Does anybody out there have a job opening for an unemployed photojournalist?

Tranquility on the Pontchartrain

At the shore's edge of the Pontchartrain
a small barren peninsula protrudes
where a lonely couple gazes toward
the lighthouse perched at its end.
Its shadow partially obstructing
the bright pallet of a setting sun.

It precariously hovers on the horizon
for one last fleeting moment.
Its hues' are awash by the mist
ascending each step of the seawall.
Just beyond, a sailing ship gracefully
glides along the crystal lake,
its sails waving a tranquil
and cherished farewell.

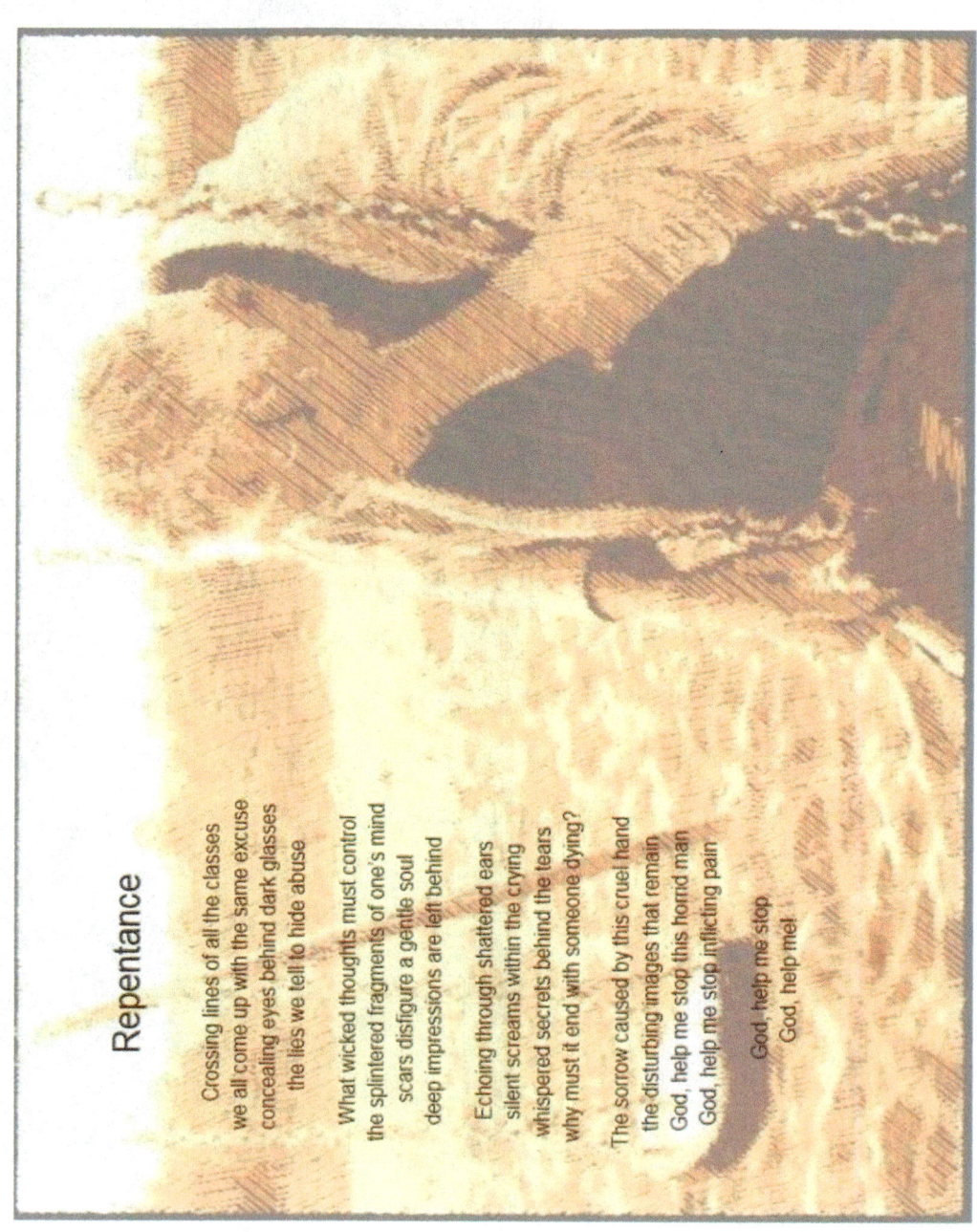

Repentance

Crossing lines of all the classes
we all come up with the same excuse
concealing eyes behind dark glasses
the lies we tell to hide abuse

What wicked thoughts must control
the splintered fragments of one's mind
scars disfigure a gentle soul
deep impressions are left behind

Echoing through shattered ears
silent screams within the crying
whispered secrets behind the tears
why must it end with someone dying?

The sorrow caused by this cruel hand
the disturbing images that remain,
God, help me stop this horrid man
God, help me stop inflicting pain

God, help me stop.
God, help me!

Writer's Block

I'm on a treacherous journey down a barren mind,
a cavernous abyss of unintelligible revelations,
void of any comprehensible inspiration.
I am perpetually staring at a blank canvas,
Continually foraging for that illusive phrase,
ransacking my hollow coffers of recollection.
Parchment decomposes from abandonment,
as does the ink drying in the quill.
There is rumbling from within,
fermenting familiar reminiscences.
Might this evoke envisions of my opus,
or the rancid sustenance I have consumed?

All Tripped Out

For over nine months I've been wedged in behind
a Houdini contraption made to keep me confined.
No more Nuns with their paddles, no more spinach and peas,
no more girls dressed in plaid with skirts way past their knees.
It'll be jeans every day, no more khaki to wear,
the school could fall down, I just couldn't care.
We were taking a trip and ready to go,
the location, a secret only our parents would know.
As we started to leave there was this terrible sound,
that came from the bumper as it dragged on the ground
from all of the luggage on top of the rack
and all of the kids that were stuffed in the back.
We were now on our way, everything was just fine,
until we all started squirming, this was not a good sign.
We played all the games and sang every song,
each kid took their turn to ask Dad, "HOW LONG?"
With all of us asking which way we were bound,
far down the road, Dad got all turned around.
Things sure looked familiar, and soon we would learn,
our sister, "THE NAVIGATOR," had made a wrong turn.
A road sign read lodging was five miles away,
it was time for a break; we'd been driving all day.

A bright green hotel was ahead on the right,
Dad needed a rest, so we stopped for the night.
We put on our suits and took over the pool,
all of us jumping and acting the fool.
We lost track of the youngest, he just couldn't be found,
he was under the water, we thought he had drowned.
Mom was upset, but he was all right,
we couldn't go swimming the rest of the night.
The next day was boring, with nothing to do,
we counted bottles of beer and cars that were blue.
"The secret is out," was all that was said,
the Great Ruby Falls was just right ahead.
One of my sisters was going out of her mind,
because her and the youngest had to be left behind.
We went down a long shaft and over a ramp,
deep underground in a cave that was damp.
Someone was screaming, "I blame this on you!"
A sister of mine had just lost her shoe.
We were now in pitch darkness, all standing around,
cupping our ears from a deafening sound.
The rushing of water was all we could hear,
with a blast of a spot light, the falls would appear.
To a really young child, it's enormously real,
but my brother was asking, "What's the big deal?

A faucet of water, maybe thirty feet tall,
what's the attraction? This is nothing at all."
Rock City was next on our journey that day,
as we stood there in line, we heard someone say,
"Beware of the Squeeze, you're gonna get stuck!"
We got through with ease, but my Dad, no such luck.
We were scratching our heads, when it started to rain,
Dad got soaking wet, but he didn't complain.
He finally got loose, and our next destination
was a four hour drive to an Indian Reservation.
You would think by now, our parents would know
not to buy us all outfits equipped with a bow.
We danced by the fire, all jumping around
to the beating of drums and a coyote sound.
No one got hurt or stuck in the eye
with all of the arrows we shot in the sky.
After that week, with ten kids in tow,
the gray in Dad's hair really started to show.
With all of the memories fresh in my head,
"I can't wait till next year," was all that I said.
As my Dad threw his hands up to the sky,
for the first time in my life, I saw that man cry.

Deserted Fragments

I stand alone pondering my existence,
my mind twisted, lost within my consciousness,
searching for memories soon forgotten.
  I wrestle to obtain my own reality,
  remembrances far from within my grasp.
Mundane thoughts elude my comprehension,
so minuscule, they transcend my ability to process.
My lapse of perception, the deserted fragments of my life,
queries of justification for my abandoned memories.
Why has this affliction absorbed my yesterdays?
  Why does it control my being, my soul,
  everything that once was my individuality?
I sit bewildered, my revelations scrolled on parchment,
  attempting to preserve my own identity.
I futilely critique each line for my idiosyncrasies,
searching for my existence within my own words.

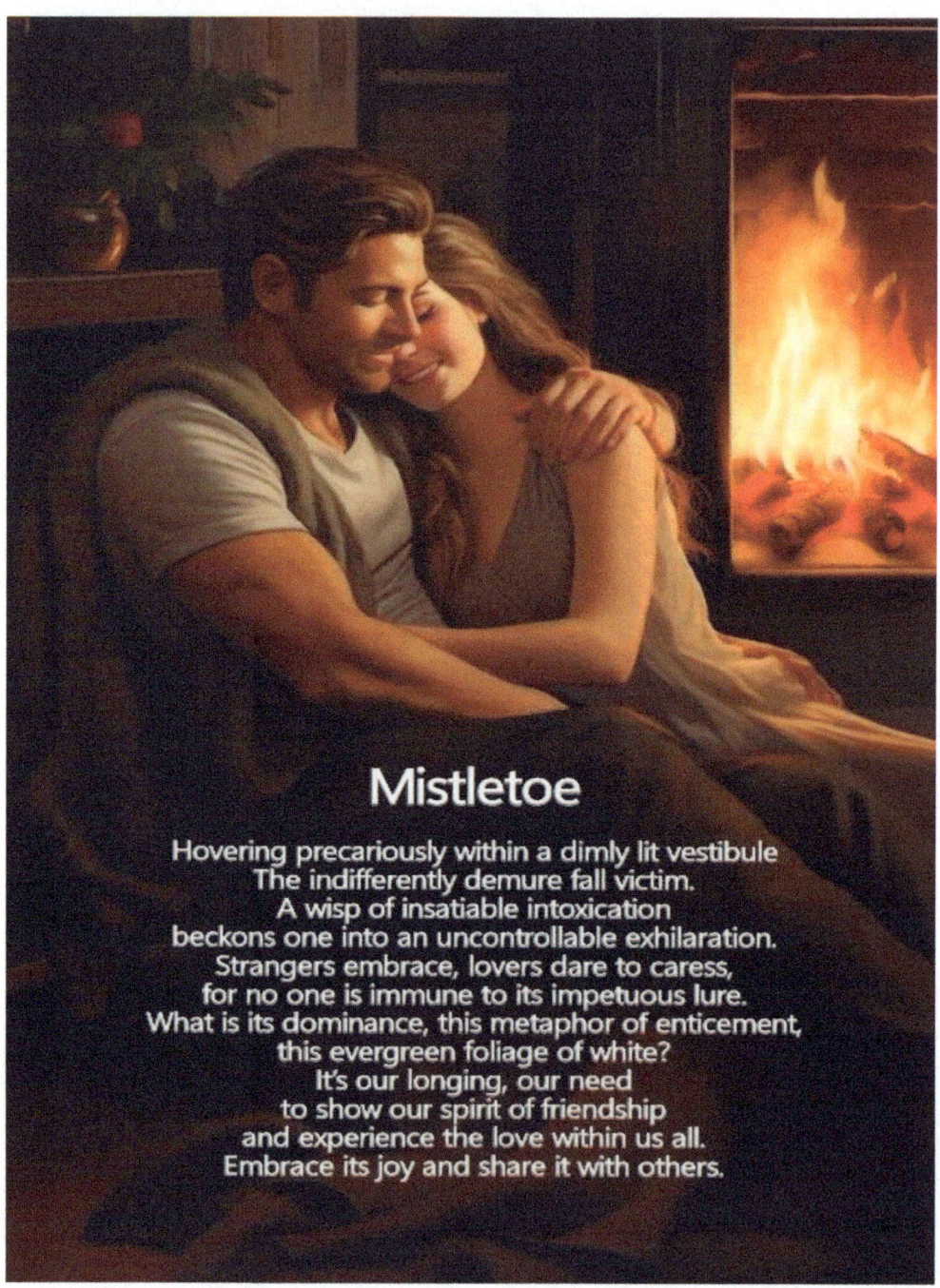

Mistletoe

Hovering precariously within a dimly lit vestibule
The indifferently demure fall victim.
A wisp of insatiable intoxication
beckons one into an uncontrollable exhilaration.
Strangers embrace, lovers dare to caress,
for no one is immune to its impetuous lure.
What is its dominance, this metaphor of enticement,
this evergreen foliage of white?
It's our longing, our need
to show our spirit of friendship
and experience the love within us all.
Embrace its joy and share it with others.

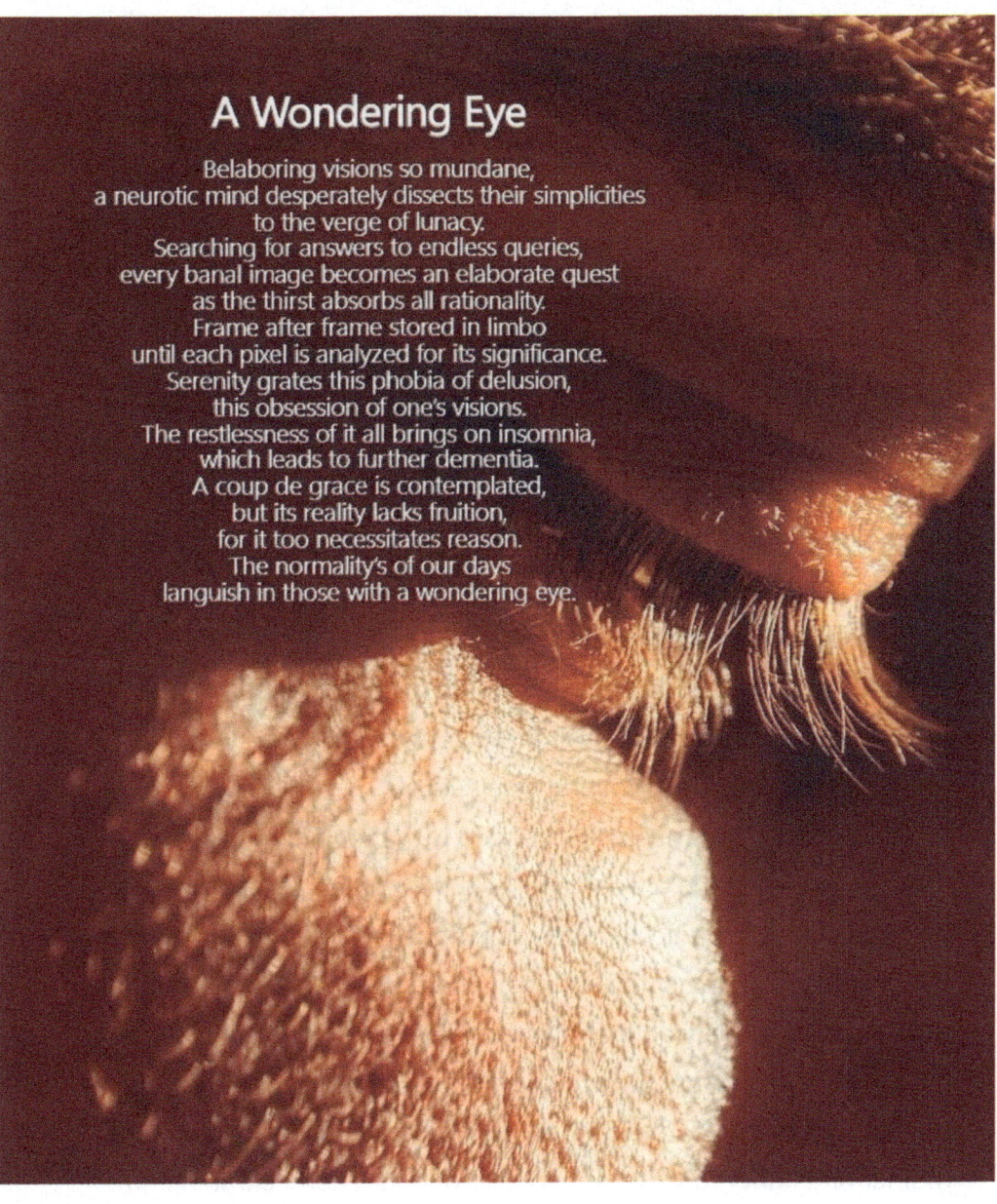

A Wondering Eye

Belaboring visions so mundane,
a neurotic mind desperately dissects their simplicities
to the verge of lunacy.
Searching for answers to endless queries,
every banal image becomes an elaborate quest
as the thirst absorbs all rationality.
Frame after frame stored in limbo
until each pixel is analyzed for its significance.
Serenity grates this phobia of delusion,
this obsession of one's visions.
The restlessness of it all brings on insomnia,
which leads to further dementia.
A coup de grace is contemplated,
but its reality lacks fruition,
for it too necessitates reason.
The normality's of our days
languish in those with a wondering eye.

Craig Mahler

Tattered Edges

I had always heard that there's a certain instant, an exact moment in everyone's life that alters their perception of their own humanity. I know that everything we do changes our lives, but this is not like winning the lottery, it's something way beyond that. For some people it's a vision, for others it's a near-death experience. For me, it was among the worn pages of a weathered scrapbook.

I'd always thought that I had lived a relatively normal middle class life. I grew up an only child to two wonderful parents. My father taught Social Studies at the local high school until his death seven years ago. My mother, who has lived in the same house for the past forty years, was a homemaker. I guess you can say she still is. Throughout my life they never pushed me to do anything I didn't want to do. They gently encouraged me to do my best. Even when I decided to quit college half way through my senior year to start working in construction, nothing was said.

Since my father's passing, I've tried to watch over my mother. I visit her at least twice a week and take her out to eat as often as possible. On one particular afternoon I had walked into her house to find her sitting on the sofa weeping. There was a letter in her hand from a lawyer explaining that her younger sister, my Aunt Vera, had died in her sleep. Aunt Vera was eight years younger than my mother and only fourteen years old when their parents passed away. My mother and father took Vera in to take of her. Then I came along.

Aunt Vera was like a big sister to me. She used to baby sit me and as I grew up she used to go with my parents to all of my sporting activities. She never married, and I

Can't, to the life of me remember ever seeing her go out on a date. Then, not long after I graduated from high school, she moved away. My mother said after an argument with Aunt Vera she decided it would be better if Aunt Vera moved out on her own. So she did, she moved all the way to Florida. After that Vera never called or visited. Our only correspondences were birthday and holiday cards to me, not my parents. The last time I saw her alive was some fifteen years ago.

My mother asked me to accompany her on the trip to Vera's home to help with some boxes Vera had left for her. When we arrived, I was surprised at the condition of the house. The grass looked as if it hadn't been cut in years and the house was in deplorable shape. We carefully entered and started searching each room for the boxes she had left. The floor creaked with our every step. A pale light filtered through the thin shear curtains revealing the sparseness of her dwelling. Torn wallpaper hung from bare walls. As bad a condition it was in, the house was immaculate. Not one speck of dust could be found.

We finally reached one of the back rooms, and there in the corner, next to a bed, were three plain cardboard boxes with my mother's name on them. As I started to lift them up, the bottom of one of the boxes fell apart. All of its contents fell to the floor. Scrapbooks, the boxes were filled with scrapbooks. My mother hurriedly picked up a few of the books and ran out of the room. I had never seen my mother in such a state, so I followed her into the living room. There, I found her weeping, on the floor, hunched over trying to hide the books from my view. Without a word, she reached for my hand and pulled me to the floor next to her. She opened one of the frayed books and handed it to me. There before me was my life, literally. Everything from faded newspaper clippings to old class photos. Why did the fact that Aunt Vera had scrapbooks of me be so upsetting to my mother? I was Vera's only relative besides my mother, and I truly believe she loved me. So why wouldn't she have kept such things?

Then I noticed a small piece of parchment sticking out from behind one of the photos. It was yellowed and brittle from age and its tattered edges crumbled in my hands as I carefully tried to unfold it. This is when I realized, this was to be my certain moment, the exact instant that would change my life from then on. It was my birth certificate. But something wasn't right. There was a mistake. But it wasn't a mistake, Vera was my birth mother.

The paper fell from my hands as the only mother I"ve ever known tried to explain that her sister had become pregnant soon after moving into my parents home. Because of the times and her age, Vera decided to let my parents take care of me. So, for the rest of their lives, they all lived with a secret they just couldn't bare to reveal. After my graduation, Vera wanted to tell me the truth, but my parents disagreed. They saw no reason to upset my life.

Surprisingly, I wasn't upset. But now I have a new perspective of who I am and who I'm meant to be. My new vision has guided me to return and finish college. I'm proud to say that I have opened a small care center where we support young unwed expecting women who can't take care of themselves. There are photos of the women we have helped on three walls of my office; on the other, hangs only two frames. In one of the frames there's a photo of my parents, all three of them. In the other, there's an old faded piece of parchment, with its tattered edges, reminding me who I was and who I need to be.

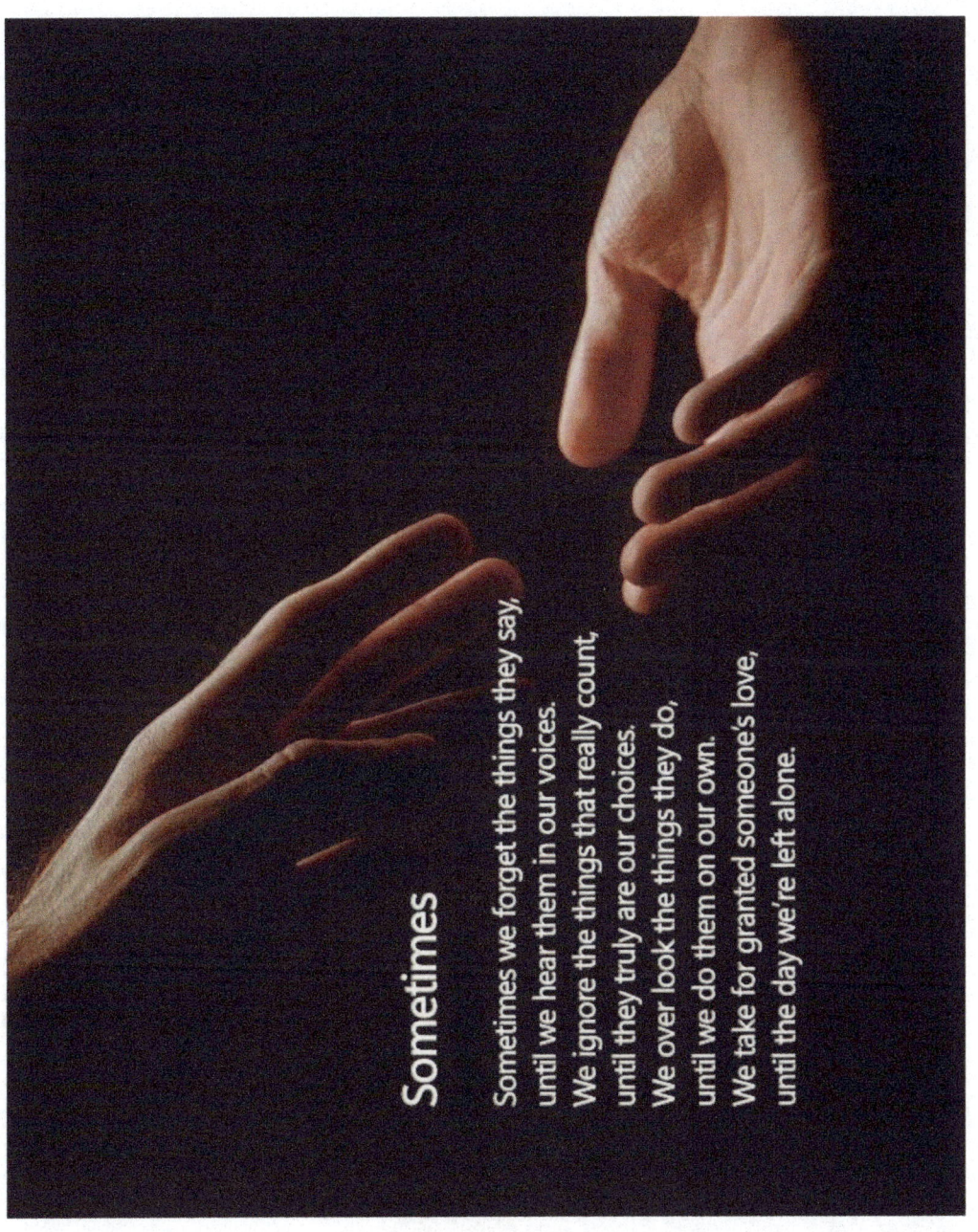

Sometimes

Sometimes we forget the things they say,
until we hear them in our voices.
We ignore the things that really count,
until they truly are our choices.
We over look the things they do,
until we do them on our own.
We take for granted someone's love,
until the day we're left alone.

Manchac Cypress

I once towered proudly over my siblings,
my moss laden arms strained
to shadow those who slumbered in my shade.
My body thick from the years,
stretching to the heavens,
soaking in its nourishment.
From within my dense blanket
I have harbored miracles of life.

I have weathered the seasons,
but now I am poised in solitude.
Limbs, once strong, wither.
I am but a fragile skeleton,
my foundation slowly wasting
from the brackish flow eroding my knees.
My body no longer supporting life
as I slowly decay into the marsh.

Nocturnal de Vieux Carre'
Werewolves of the French Quarter

Not yet long into the night, a translucent mist hovers,
cold as it settles upon the fine hairs.
Runty knobs form along the exposed skin,
an insufferable chill has come to the Quarter.
Secured dwellings, sheltering those from who prey in the dark,
prowling the vulnerable, pilfering life from the innocent.
Gas streetlights lay witness to this harrowing theater,
stretching shadows, slithering the alleys for a pristine morsel.
Moist from a recent offering, hunger demands fruition,
devouring the still beating heart prolongs one's existence.
Gnawing at the bone, consuming of the flesh,
ensuring nourishment 'til the next illuminating full Luna.
Before the dawn reveals this carnage of the night,
a solitary horse-drawn cart wanders the curbs,
collecting the discarded remains of those ravaged,
harboring the rumors only locals know to be true.
Awaiting the ensuing engorged orb,
I endure, I thirst, I hunger.

My Trip to the Zoo

I have to tell you before I begin,
this story turns out okay in the end.
As a boy from the city, at the young age of five,
I had never before seen wild animals alive.
I had to find out if the stories were true,
you could see all the animals, at a place called the Zoo.
We were walking around and hadn't been there that long,
even at my young age, I knew something was wrong.
My brothers and sisters all knew what I meant,
my Dad got upset at all the money he spent.
This place really stunk, and it wasn't the smell,
there were dark gloomy cages, a primitive hell.
God's creatures, in prison, with nothing to do,
stuck behind bars for humans to view.
We watched how they lived; it was making us sad,
the more that we studied, the more we got mad.

Not one little thing resembled their home,
they had no place to play, nowhere to roam.
The only things we enjoyed on our visit that day,
was sitting for hours watching the Sea Lions play.
We enjoyed our time rolling down Old Monkey Hill,
everything else there was making us ill.
Decades have passed since that first trip I took,
I've gone back since then, to take a new look.
I was pleasantly surprised at the changes they did,
the prison was gone that I saw as a kid.
There are none of the cages they had in the past,
it's an animal oasis; they can roam free at last.
With my children it tow, I take them to see,
an animal's life and how it should be.
Now, when I visit, every once in a while,
I stare at my daughter and watch the girl smile.
Watching a child, watching animals play,
the joy in their laughter, what more can I say?

The Warrington Warehouse

I passed an old landmark the other day
only known to a select few and I remembered
the weekends we all shared there together.
We were living in an easier time
than those who came before us.
It was an era without it's own identity,
just following Vietnam.
We were an odd collection of individuals
meeting every weekend in an arhaic building
located just behind Marie's Salon.
It wasn't much more than an old garage
with its tattered sofas and makeshift light show
where we would lounge about.
We would all sit around awaiting the howl of the Wolfman,
signaling the beginning of the Midnight Special.
We weren't there for the music,
you could get that anywhere.
It was the chance to spend time with your closet friends,
to listen to the same old stories
that mad you fall out of your seat.
I can't remember when we all started meeting there,
but while it lasted, it was the place to be.
The Warrington Warehouse has been closed for years now,
and it saddened me until I realized, it's not the location,
it's the friends that forever remain a part of your life.
Whenever and where ever we now meet, I hear a faint howl,
and I see the doors to that old garage
opening wide, inviting me in.

The Path

With one sweep a path has been laid, a righteous one towards the truth
that what we have and what we believe can be taken in an instant.
We know not what is before us, only where we have been,
and that it has led us here, to our crossroads.
We have been given the choice to wander in the direction of regret,
or follow the path towards our salvation.
Let our Faith guide us, for our journey has just begun.

One Final Tap for a Shining Star

...Intolerance, indifference and ignorance abounds within our society. As a race, we still haven't learned the true meaning of compassion.
 Being human doesn't make us humane, compassion does. We must embrace our humanity. Make a difference in someone else's life...
...Craig Mahler

CHAPTER ONE
Coffee and Beignets: Looking for Substance

It was a typical early summer morning in New Orleans, if there is such a thing. Humidity was at 100 percent and fog was rolling in off the Mississippi. The temperature was already reaching ninety, and it wasn't even a half past dawn. The sounds of the river echoed down the alleys of the French Quarter, only to be muffled by the clanging of plates as I sat at a corner table in the Café Du Monde. It is my usual stop each morning, and I was now on my second cup of coffee desperately trying to decide my future. I write a monthly article for a local travel magazine and I was tired of doing stories about the local landmarks. How many times can someone write about the St. Louis Cathedral or Bourbon Street?

I had just finished a story on the new War Museum in which I had added some bios of the people who work there. Or should I say Volunteers? They are all retired service men and women, proudly telling their own experiences of what happened to them during, what they described as, "The Conflict." But my so-called editor scrapped everything but the hardware, you know, the tanks, the guns and old Army uniforms. What makes the museum so interesting are the people who wear those uniforms. Their lives are what interest me, not only their war experiences, but their personal lives as well. I wanted to know what they did before and after the war, and how it affected the directions they took. But these forgotten heroes didn't seem interested in talking about anything other than their war years, which I guess was tough enough for them, knowing now what they had gone through.

I decided to go freelance, but wasn't sure which direction I should take. Lately, a lot of my fellow writers have written war novels, and most of those novels are on Generals becoming politicians. There was something different I wanted to do. That's when Willie came into my life. Or I should say; I came into his.

I was just starting my third cup of coffee, when the gentle hues of the Sun billowed over the roof of the Cabildo. Its rays illuminated the ever-dispersing mist crawling along the stone corridor surrounding the Square. An opaque beacon shot through the wrought iron fence, creating a pencil-thin stairway upon the crumbled slate walkway. I was beckoned by these imaginary steps toward the spectacle of sights, the sideshow of vendors within the confines of the Square. This is why I love this part of the city at this time of the morning. It's this type of menagerie that entices tourist and locals alike to the wonder and magic of the French Quarter.

There among the painters, fortune-tellers and performance artist was this elderly black man shining shoes. This man seemed to be out of place, yet he fit perfectly within the eclectic scheme of things. He was a slender man who looked to be in his sixties. But I would soon find out, he was actually closer to eighty. He was neatly dressed in pressed slacks and an off-white button down shirt with a thin black tie. His only tools were an old tattered brush, a rather large stained towel and a collection of assorted cans of paste. There was also an old black wooden crate where his customers could rest their feet. I sat and watched as people just passed him by, oblivious to his existence. Occasionally someone would stop, but they seemed to only want to ask him for directions. When they did stop for a shine, I would notice their interactions. Every once in a while, the shoeshine man would nod his head and utter a "yes sir" or a "no sir" and as he finished, only a "thank you." It struck me funny, that a man in his line of work would be so distant. But the customers seemed to be just as indifferent. Some would just read their newspapers and others would just stare off into space.

    This man captivated me. I had to find out why someone would choose such a profession, or had the profession chosen him? I asked my waiter about the man, and he told me that as long as he could remember, the old man had always been in that spot, shining shoes. He didn't even know the man's name, and I don't think he really cared. So, I started asking the different vendors around the Square about this man. Some didn't know the man was there. Others told me he went by the name of "Shoeshine Willie." I had always assumed that in this small community, everyone knew each other. But I guess Willie just stayed to himself. One of the vendors suggested that I check with the permit office. He said that everyone taking space around the Square has to have a permit. So, off to City Hall I went.

CHAPTER TWO
When all else fails, go to the Source

After an exhausting day searching the archives downtown, I still couldn't find what I was looking for. All I could find was this; the man's name is William C. Butler, and he lives alone in an old shotgun house in the Lower Ninth Ward. I had a friend of mine, a police officer, check his record, but it is clean as a whistle. Who is this man? What is his story? My connection at the newspaper had found a few things on a Willem D. Butler, but it definitely wasn't Willie. That guy was a hero who passed away years ago. So, I decided to go right to the source itself, Willie.

With the most scuffed up pair of shoes I could find now planted on my feet, I headed back to the Quarter, in my quest of Willie. When I arrived, Willie was already hard at work. As I waited my turn, I noticed his artistry. Like a dancer waltzing across a ballroom floor, Willie's hands moved gracefully from side to side and back and forth around his customer's feet. Almost as soon as he had started his work, he was finished. Willie's customer looked down and grunted what seemed to be an approval, then dropped a five-dollar bill toward Willie's outstretched hands.

It was now my turn and I put one foot up on the rise so that Willie could begin. This was my first opportunity to see him up close. His face was worn by the Sun and his hands seemed to be permanently stained from all the years of doing his trade. Without a word, Willie grabbed his can of black paste and reached for my shoe.
All of a sudden, Willie stopped and stared up at me. He knew something wasn't right. Willie told me, in all his years of shining

shoes; he had never seen a pair look so bad. So I broke down and told him my plan. I explained to him how I was interested in interviewing him for a story I wanted to write. He thought about it for a few minutes, and then decided it was okay. His only request was that we do it away from his work. I told him I would pay him for his time, but Willie didn't want my money. He did say he would accept lunch, on me of course. So just around noon, Willie and I went off to a nearby café. And as Willie would eat, he would pause momentarily between bites of his pasta to tell his story.

Some eight decades ago, when he was just about six years old, Willie would sit and watch, as his father would go about the business of shining shoes. He would observe his father's clientele, and how they ignored the man at their feet. They stood motionless, reading their papers as if no one was there. One after another, the men would put their feet up on an old crate and fade off into their own worlds. Just then, Willie stopped his story to add that a lot of things haven't changed much since those days. He was referring to his own customer's behavior, and I agreed. After another bite of his food, Willie continued on with his tale.

From early in the morning, until way past dinnertime, his father would earn nickels down on his knees, trying to bring home what he could for his family. As the years would pass, the nickels turned to dimes, and then to quarters. His father's business was steady, as long as the weather would hold out. When it was winter, there was very little to eat. No one wants to stand in the cold to get his or her shoes shined.

Willie and his older brother Travis would sometimes tap dance for pennies, as people would stroll by their father's stand. Their dancing seemed to be a hit with the tourist visiting the Quarter. But Willie's dad wanted more for his kids. He made sure they did their homework before they could dance after school. And on the weekends, they had to do their chores and go to church. Other than that, Willie and Travis could be found tapping away every afternoon and every weekend along side their father in Jackson Square.

As Willie and Travis got older, the crowds would dwindle. The novelty had run its course. When they were young kids, it was cute. But as teenagers, it looked as if they were begging. His brother got a job washing dishes at a local restaurant and Willie tried his best to finish school. At the age of fifteen Willie dropped out.

CHAPTER THREE
Pennies to Broadway: Willie's Climb

Willie only knew how to do two things, tap dancing and shining shoes. And Willie didn't want to end up like his dad, shining shoes the rest of his life. Over the next couple of years Willie waited tables, cleaned dishes and a whole array of assorted odd jobs. One day Willie joined up with a touring dance show, but not as a dancer, he was the hired help. He would set up and tear down the stages for the real ARTIST. From off stage, Willie would watch the dancers and learn all of their moves. He knew he could do a better job dancing than they ever could. But he knew in his heart he would never get the chance to show what he could do.

The next couple of years Willie would go about his work. That was, until one certain day he was spotted dancing around back stage. A Broadway producer hired Willie on the spot. He was sent to New York as an understudy for the 1937 musical, "Muddy River." For the late Nineteen-thirties, this was an ambitious show. No one had ever brought an all black musical to Broadway, and Willie was a part of it all. In the beginning Willie would only have a bit part. That was until the lead dancer broke his leg. It was Willie's turn to shine, and I don't mean shoes.

The show was a huge success, mostly due to Willie's outstanding talent. He was now a star, and with that stardom, came lots of money. And as hard as he tried, Willie couldn't help but let the fame go to his head. A lot of people in New York resented Willie's success. They didn't like the fact that a black man was living so well, no matter how famous he was. What made matters worse was that Willie was popular with the ladies. Some of them were white, and that just wasn't allowed, not in New York, not in the late Thirties. Almost every one of the ladies, white or black, were after one thing, Willie's money. He was definitely the talk of the town. And Willie could have cared less what people thought of him. He was having fun.

Willie went through his money as fast as he made it. He had lots of friends; the best money could buy. The women and the partying took its toll on Willie. He started to have his fair share of problems. When he drank, he drank way too much. And when he was drunk, he was obnoxious, which led to fights. As Willie puts it, "He got uppity." One of his biggest problems occurred when one of his girlfriends became pregnant, and she was white. They tried keeping it a secret, but in that town, there's no such thing. Even though, as they say, "she lost the baby," most of Willie's closest friends abandoned him.

This rude awakening set Willie straight. He quit everything cold turkey, the women, the partying and the booze, everything. To this day Willie says he hasn't had another drink.

Willie had just finished his lunch and asked if we could continue the interview another day. He told me he didn't work on Mondays and he asked me if I didn't mind spending that day chatting while he did his laundry. I agreed without hesitation. Willie gave me his address, which I already had, but I wouldn't tell him that. I didn't want him to know I had already checked him out. I asked him what I should bring for lunch, and look of disbelief came over his face. He asked me if I was really a native of New Orleans. You see, Monday is red beans and rice day, anybody from New Orleans knows that.

CHAPTER FOUR
A Mess Private's private mess

I arrived at Willie's house bright and early that next Monday morning. It was 8:00 a.m. and Willie was already on his second load of clothes. There was a pot of beans soaking in the kitchen and Willie was on his porch folding towels. I asked him if I could help him with anything and he said I would probably just mess things up. There was something about Willie's weird sense of humor. You just couldn't tell if he was kidding you or not. He could be putting you down or giving you a compliment, you just didn't know. Willie told me to stay put, so I did. He went into his house and stayed for what seemed like an hour, but it wasn't more than a couple of minutes. I must say, in his neighborhood, a white man sitting on a porch is not a common site. A lot of people seemed to purposely walk up and down the sidewalk slowly, real slowly. I was starting to get a little nervous. Okay, I was scared to death. That's when Willie came back out with a big pitcher of iced tea. And as soon as he sat down, he started telling his story from right where he had left off.

In 1939, Willie got the opportunity to star in the movie version of "Muddy River." So he hopped on a train and headed to California. On his westward journey he met a beautiful young girl named Martha. He first noticed her as he passed through the dining car. She was trying to get something to eat. Blacks weren't allowed in the "white's only" car. I keep forgetting how it was for African-Americans back then. But Willie was quick to remind me, "Things haven't changed all that much since then."

He invited Martha to have dinner with him, in his room, and she accepted. Over dinner, Willie found out Martha was going to live with her aunt and uncle in Los Angeles. Her mother had passed away and Martha's father didn't think the partying atmosphere of Harlem was the place for a single young girl. Besides, she had just made eighteen and wanted to see if things were any better on the West Coast. Willie and Martha seemed to hit it off right away. She became infatuated with Willie. She had met someone famous, and was surprised that he was really a nice guy. Willie was struck by Martha's beauty and overall innocence. The three-day journey ended with Martha inviting Willie to meet her aunt and uncle. They approved of Martha and Willie's relationship, and soon after he finished his movie, they got married. Willie was on cloud nine. He had a wonderful wife and his movie career had taken off. He was in high demand. Almost every movie musical, black or white, had Willie starring in it.

Willie and Martha bought a new house near Hollywood, or as near to it as they were allowed. But they were doing just fine where they were. They entertained their friends with lavish dinner parties and hit all the exclusive hot stops. Even the ones normally reserved for whites. At this point, Willie modestly described himself as an early Sammy Davis Jr.

Everything was going along just fine, until a familiar pattern started to appear. This time it was Martha. With all the partying, she had developed a drinking problem. Willie tried to help, but it only made things worse. He was getting frustrated by the fact that he had kicked his habit so fast, yet she couldn't. What complicated things even worse, was that he wasn't always around to help. Willie was gone for weeks doing his movies. He finally decided to take time off from acting, but by then, she was already too far-gone. Watching over

Martha became impossible; she would just hide bottles around the house. When he did have to leave the house, Willie would lock her in the bedroom. But she would just climb out of the window and head to the nearest bar.

He finally took her to a hospital for help. But back then; they didn't have the treatment centers like today. They basically locked you up for months until they thought you were better. When they finally let her out, Martha was a completely different person, and I don't mean for the better. She could never forgive Willie for what he had done to her, even if it was for her own good.

Two months later, the Japanese bombed Pearl Harbor. Willie thought he would do his part for his country, as did the other stars, by trying to push War Bonds. But the Army had other plans for Willie. He was drafted. Willie was going to serve his country, but not with a gun. He was going to serve with a knife; a kitchen knife. Willie was stationed as a cook on an island somewhere in the South Pacific. But that didn't bother Willie; he was doing what his country wanted him to do. Besides, after the war he would be back in front of the cameras again.

CHAPTER FIVE
Sec. B pg. 08: Colored Actor gets Medal

How could Willie have known just how things would change after the war? When Willie returned to the states, his life would start a fast decline. Martha had left him and took all of his money. What made matters worse was that Hollywood wasn't making musicals anymore. There was no place for a tap dancing black man in a War movie. So Willie tried Broadway again, but they didn't want him either. They felt as if he had abandoned the stage when he left for the movies. Willie was left with only one choice. He had to move back to New Orleans.

Things weren't any better when Willie got back. He found his father still shining shoes in the Quarter. All the money Willie had sent home over the years was gambled away by his brother. Willie's father had never told him what Travis had done. Willie had to find out from the neighbors. You see, while Willie was off at war, he had heard Travis had been found dead in the streets. He now knew it was because of the gambling debts Travis owed.

Willie abruptly stopped telling his story, saying he had to check on the red beans in the kitchen. But I knew better. As I followed him into the house, I watched as Willie wiped the tears from his eyes. I respectfully stayed in the living room, giving Willie some time to himself. I took this opportunity to look around.

Willie's house was sparsely decorated with very little hanging on the walls. But one thing did catch my eye. There before me was a newspaper article about Willie. And as I read it, I came to realize why Willie had been walking with a limp. I had assumed it was because of his age, but this brief article explained a lot. Willie was a hero. He had received a medal. Not just any medal, Willie had been awarded the Congressional Medal of Honor, this nation's highest honor. And Willie had received it from the President of the United States. I was amazed at what I read and appalled by its length. The whole article couldn't have been more than fifty words long. And it was stuck way back in the middle of Section B. Today, this would be front-page news.

Just then I realized Willie was standing behind me. I apologized for my snooping, but Willie just laughed. He wanted me to see it. Willie knew what he was doing. He knew I couldn't have passed it up. So I just had to ask, "What's with the Medal?" With that, we headed back out to the porch where he continued to enlighten me.

Within less than six years, Willie had gone full circle. He was back tap dancing on the streets of New Orleans for whatever loose change a stranger would offer. Willie struggled for the next couple of years, taking any job he could get. That was until the Korean War, when Willie signed up, this time as a fighting soldier.

He was assigned to a forward company. Their duty was to clear the way for all the troops that would follow behind them. On one particular mission, Willie's company was ambushed, and four of his fellow soldiers were gunned down. The rest of the men were trapped and surrounded by the enemy. For more than six hours they battled within a fierce firestorm, waiting for reinforcements, but none would arrive.

One by one, they were getting picked off by sniper fire. Willie could hear the whistling of the bullets as they passed inches from his head. He could hear the screams for help, as each shot would hit its mark. Willie had to do something. He had to get those men out of there. So Willie crawled on his belly toward the nearest screams.

There he found his first wounded soldier. He grabbed the man by the back of his vest and dragged him two miles to safety. Without any hesitation, Willie returned for the others. He had pulled out six men that night, two after being wounded himself. Willie was shot in the leg, which he ended up losing.

    I asked Willie about it, and he said, "You know, all my life I was a dancer. At first it was hard, knowing that for the rest of your life you will never be able to do what you love to do. But over time you face reality and move on." So that's exactly what he did.

CHAPTER SIX
Among the Rising Tide

For many years you could find Willie at his father's side, shining shoes. And after his father passed away, Willie would continue on by himself. For the next thirty-five years Willie would politely say his yes sirs and no sirs, just as his dad had done all his life. The customers would read their papers and ignore him just as others had done to his father for so many years. Every once in a while, some elderly tourist would ask Willie about the little Negro boy that used to dance here, long ago. And Willie would tell them that the boy grew up to be a big movie star, never leading on that he was that boy. I guess his pride kept him from revealing the truth.

I asked Willie why he didn't strike up conversations with his customers while he was shining their shoes. He was obviously a friendly talkative person. Willie was quick to reply, "I have a lot more conversations with the tourist asking for directions than I do with my customers. They just seem to like it that way." Then he told me my constant questioning was messing him up. But I wasn't messing up his story telling. I was screwing up his concentration while he was trying to separate his socks. I figured out much later that Willie was pulling my leg. Every sock that Willie owned was exactly alike. After I apologized for interrupting, I asked him to continue. He just started laughing. That was it. Willie was done. His story was at its end, so I thought.

I spent the next six months of my life a self imposed hermit, purposely sheltering myself from every miniscule distraction. I sat among piles of wasted paper, each wad representing a failed attempt

Craig Mahler 75

to serve justice to this man. A man I now consider the most descent forgotten Hero a society could have ever allowed to slip into the darkness, an abyss of loneliness. This shame has fallen upon my shoulders and I had the power in me to right this wrong, if only the words would flow from the now drying matter wedged between my ears.

I sat in my small apartment, day after day, reading my notes, these words of my new friend. Not "*THESE WORDS*", but HIS WORDS! How could I tell the story he so beautifully described to me, than to use his words? Word for word, I feverously typed away, this autobiography Willie unwittingly dictated to me.

Just as I was finishing my lengthy acknowledgment and loving postscript to this tribute, my neighbor busted down my door. I had evidently missed the fact that a hurricane was bearing down on New Orleans, TODAY! I grabbed my laptop and my keys and headed for Memphis. There I hooked up with an agent who got me a deal with a publisher.

In all of the confusion of the hurricane and the excitement of publishing the book, I had forgotten one thing, Willie. I tried calling, but Willie's phone had been disconnected. I called everyone I could think of that might know something, but got nowhere. I got on the next available flight back to New Orleans and began my search for my dear friend. Sitting alone, within that crowded airplane, I realized that I had become just like everyone else who had ignored Willie. In my zest to write his story, I selfishly abandoned my friend.

As soon I got back into town, I immediately headed for Willie's home. As I drove closer, passing through the flood-ravished neighborhood, my heart sank further in my chest. When I turned the corner towards his house, or what was left of it, I knew it wasn't going to be good. I squeezed past the mildewed plywood covering the opening where Willie's front door used to be. The droplets of my tears formed a path through this dilapidated ruin. I was looking for a sign that would lead me to Willie. I found my answer on the wall. It was the framed article of when Willie received his medal. Hanging next to it, on a rusted nail, were a pair Willie's old tap shoes. I knew he wouldn't have left these things behind. Still, this was the beginning of my quest. I had to find out what had happened to my friend. I was sure someone at Jackson Square would know something, but no one did.

CHAPTER SEVEN
One Final Dance; Saying Farewell

There I sat, drinking my third cup of coffee, slumped over the same old table outside Cafe de Monde where this story all began. I was no closer to finding my friend when I heard someone ask about the old shoeshine guy from the square. The reply took my breath away. This person said he had read an obituary about how Willie had made it to Memphis, where he passed away of a heart attack, just last week.

He died alone, and I blamed myself. I could have done something, but I was too selfish, worried about getting a book deal. Well, I was determined to make this right. I went back to Willie's place and gathered what I could. I donated the items and all of the proceeds from the book to the War Museum for a Memorial to honor Willie.

For the past two years I've been volunteering as a guide at the museum. Just today I was talking with a young group of students touring the museum. They listened intensely as I told them about a platoon of soldiers who were about to embark on a mission, for many of them, their last. As I continued, one of the students stopped me to ask why there was an old pair of tap shoes among all of the war memorabilia. I proudly started telling them the story of "Shoeshine Willie" Butler. I pictured Willie in my mind and I unconsciously started to dance. I guess it was my way of honoring this special hero, this shining star. It was my chance to give Willie the final taps he deserved.

In these vast somber halls, the last thing I expected to hear was laughter. I looked around and there before me, amongst these applauding young admirers, stood Willie. He had a huge grin across his face, telling these kids, as usual, I was messing it all up. And as Willie and I tearfully embraced, he explained where he had been.

After thinking about where his life had led him, Willie said he wasn't quite ready to call it quits. He had met some big-wig in Memphis who actually knew who he was. In fact, he was a fan. This guy gave Willie a ticket to New York and a shot to audition for a part in the Broadway revival of Muddy River. Though it was a small part, it did garner him a nomination for a Tony. There's even talk of a new movie version.

Willie playfully asked, "Is an Oscar to much to ask for?"

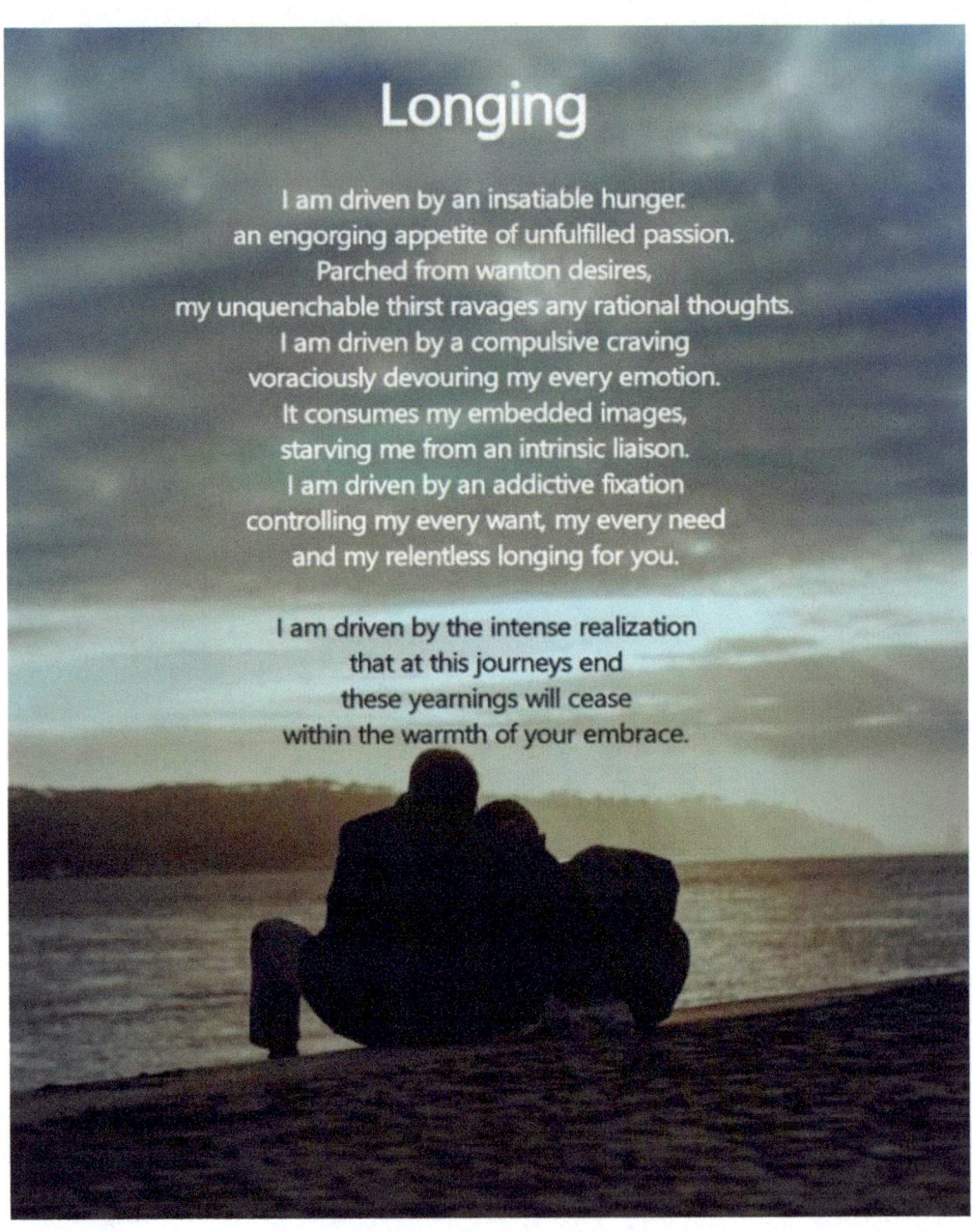

Reunion of Strangers – Love in Waiting

How times changes the things I remember,
the nights embracing your thoughts,
the warmth within your eyes
and the gentleness of your touch.
These memories lost to time,
The one's I never really knew.
Lover's meeting, a cautious encounter,
one that may never had been
but for a reunion of strangers.
Cordial exchanges, thirty years lost,
destiny has led us to this union of souls.
Two Hearts, no longer love in waiting,
creating memories together,
to be shared as one,
as it was always meant to be.

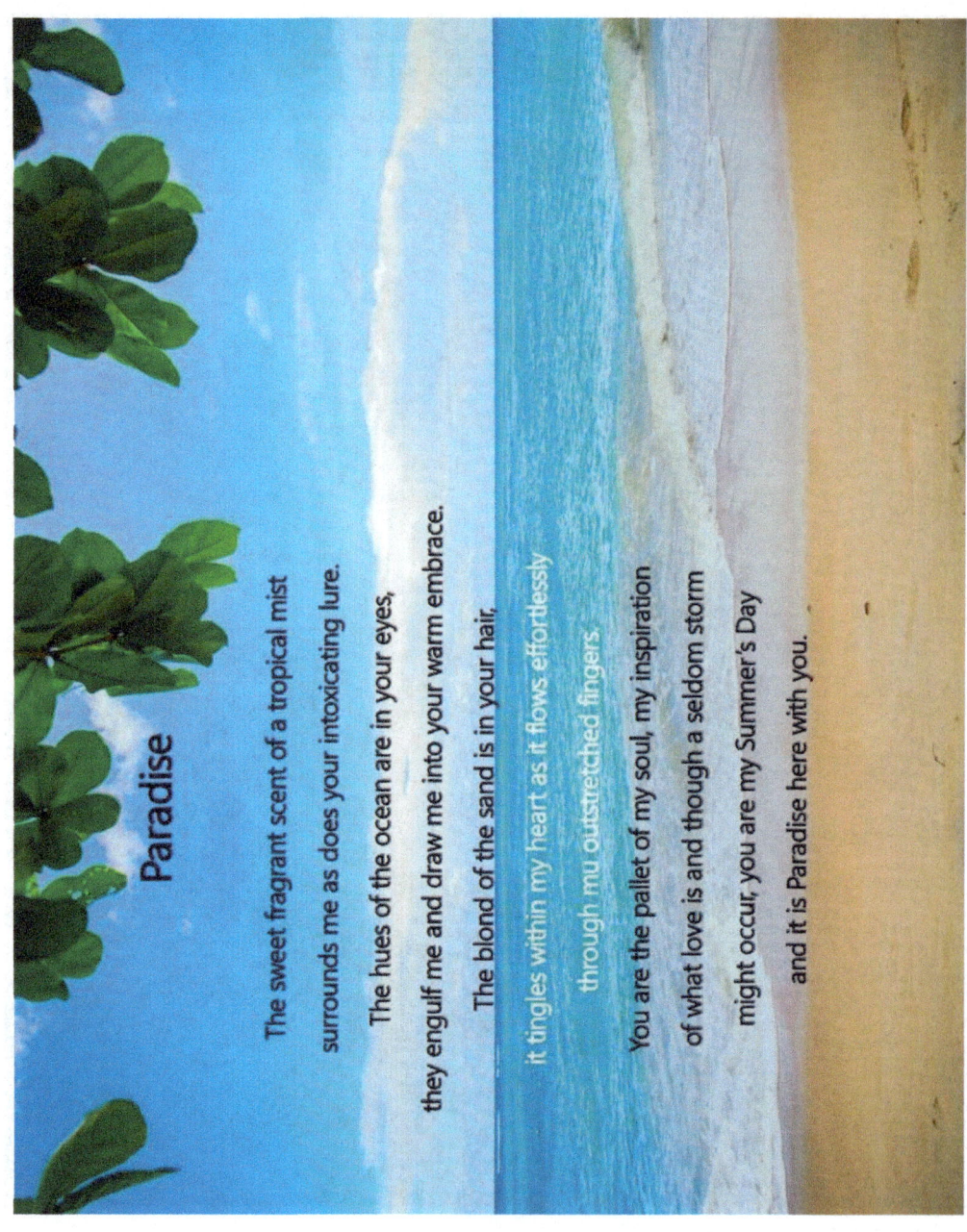

Paradise

The sweet fragrant scent of a tropical mist
surrounds me as does your intoxicating lure.

The hues of the ocean are in your eyes,
they engulf me and draw me into your warm embrace.

The blond of the sand is in your hair,
it tingles within my heart as it flows effortlessly
through my outstretched fingers.

You are the pallet of my soul, my inspiration
of what love is and though a seldom storm
might occur, you are my Summer's Day
and it is Paradise here with you.

Made in the USA
Coppell, TX
17 June 2024

33620059R10049